ISBN-13:978-1482691276
ISBN-10:1482691272
Story by Barbara Miller
Book Illustrations by Inga Shalvashvili
Book Design by Adrian Navarrete

Lily Lemon Blossom
Safari Friends

Story by Barbara Miller
Illustrations by Inga Shalvashvili

Lily received wildlife pictures from her aunt Fran, who explores faraway places, in faraway lands.

So right away Lily starts making plans, to have her very own adventure in her own faraway land.

She bunny and teddy sat on the front porch in the shade, thinking and planning and drinking lemonade.

"Where should we go to take pictures
to show aunt Fran? Maybe giraffe
would like the hot desert sands.

Or maybe a safari trip where the big animals are? Oh yes, we'll go there, It's not very far."

Lily worked very hard getting everything ready. She dressed herself for the trip, then bunny and then teddy.

They stepped off the front
porch into safari land.
They crept very slowly
with camera in hand.

They parted some bushes and not making a sound, saw a family of lions asleep on the ground.

They took a
picture and hurried
away, to the sounds of
happy chattering and play.

In the tall tree at the
end of the road, they
saw monkeys jumping,
flipping and hanging
by their toes.

The little monkeys loved
having their pictures taken
by Lily. They chatted and
giggled and were ever so silly.

She took pictures of lions
and bears having fun, as
they watched Millie the
snake dancing in the sun.

Click, click, went the
camera as they stood
behind a tree.

"These are going to be great," said Lily, as bunny hid from a bee.

They took pictures of elephants and zebras walking together, birds flying over their heads with the prettiest of feathers.

Ants happily marching in the shade. With captain ant proudly leading the parade.

She took one last picture of her
friends all together. This one she
will keep, forever and ever.

The sun will be setting
soon so they packed up to leave.
"We have many beautiful pictures,"
said Lily. "I think aunt Fran will
be pleased."

"Come teddy, come bunny we can no longer stay. Goodbye safari friends, we'll visit soon another day."

The End